STAMPEDE OF THE EDMONTOSAURUS

DINOSAUR COVE™

STAMPEDE OF THE EDMONTOSAURUS

BY
REX STONE

ILLUSTRATED BY
MIKE SPOOR

SCHOLASTIC INC.

New York Toronto London Auckland Sydney
Mexico City New Delhi Hong Kong Buenos Aires

**WITH SPECIAL THANKS TO JAN BORCHETT
AND SARA VOGLER
THANK YOU, ALSO, TO MARK FORD OF THE BRITISH
AND IRISH METEORITE SOCIETY FOR HIS PATIENT
AND HELPFUL ADVICE.
FOR GRANDPA DILLON—R.S.
THESE ILLUSTRATIONS ARE FOR YOU, CHRISTOPHER.
ENJOY THE ADVENTURE!—M.S.**

No part of this publication may be reproduced, stored in a retrieval system, or transmitted in any form or by any means, electronic, mechanical, photocopying, recording, or otherwise, without written permission of the publisher. For information regarding permission, write to Working Partners Ltd., Stanley House, St. Chad's Place, London WC1X 9HH, United Kingdom.

ISBN-13: 978-0-545-05382-2
ISBN-10: 0-545-05382-X

Published by Scholastic Inc., 557 Broadway,
New York, NY 10012, by arrangement with Working Partners Ltd.
SCHOLASTIC, LITTLE APPLE, and associated logos are trademarks and/or registered trademarks of Scholastic Inc. DINOSAUR COVE is a registered trademark of Working Partners Ltd.

12 11 10 9 8   11 12 13 14/0

Printed in the U.S.A.
First printing, April 2009

FACT FILE

➡️ JAMIE HAS JUST MOVED FROM THE CITY TO LIVE IN THE LIGHTHOUSE IN DINOSAUR COVE. JAMIE'S DAD IS OPENING A DINOSAUR MUSEUM ON THE BOTTOM FLOOR OF THE LIGHTHOUSE. WHEN JAMIE GOES HUNTING FOR FOSSILS IN THE CRUMBLING CLIFFS ON THE BEACH, HE MEETS A LOCAL BOY, TOM, AND THE TWO DISCOVER AN AMAZING SECRET: A WORLD WITH REAL, LIVE DINOSAURS! BUT THE BOYS HAVE TO WATCH OUT FOR FALLING OBJECTS AND STAMPEDES!

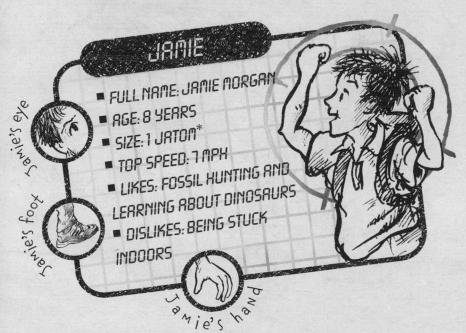

JAMIE

- FULL NAME: JAMIE MORGAN
- AGE: 8 YEARS
- SIZE: 1 JATOM*
- TOP SPEED: 7 MPH
- LIKES: FOSSIL HUNTING AND LEARNING ABOUT DINOSAURS
- DISLIKES: BEING STUCK INDOORS

Jamie's eye

Jamie's foot

Jamie's hand

*NOTE: A JATOM IS THE SIZE OF JAMIE OR TOM: 4 FT TALL AND 60 LBS IN WEIGHT.

TOM

- FULL NAME: THOMAS CLAY
- AGE: 8 YEARS
- SIZE: 1 JATOM*
- TOP SPEED: 7 MPH
- LIKES: TRACKING ANIMALS AND EXPLORING WILDLIFE
- DISLIKES: RAINY DAYS

Tom's eye   Tom's hand

WANNA

- FULL NAME: WANNANOSAURUS
- AGE: 65 – 80 MILLION YEARS**
- SIZE: LESS THAN A JATOM*
- TOP SPEED: 30 MPH, ESPECIALLY WHEN BEING CHASED BY A T-REX
- LIKES: STINKY GINKGO FRUIT AND BANGING HIS HEAD ON TREE TRUNKS
- DISLIKES: SCARY DINOSAURS

Wanna's head   Wanna's foot

*NOTE: A JATOM IS THE SIZE OF JAMIE OR TOM: 4 FT TALL AND 60 LBS IN WEIGHT.
**NOTE: SCIENTISTS CALL THIS PERIOD THE LATE CRETACEOUS.

EDMONTOSAURUS

Edmontosaurus's hoof

Edmontosaurus's eye

Edmontosaurus's teeth

Edmontosaurus's nose

- FULL NAME: EDMONTOSAURUS
- AGE: 65 – 80 MILLION YEARS**
- LENGTH: 10 JATOMS*
- WEIGHT: 130 JATOMS*
- TOP SPEED: ABOUT 28 MPH ON FOUR LEGS
- LIKES: THE FOREST, WHERE IT CAN HIDE FROM PREDATORS AND SNACK, TOO
- DISLIKES: BEING ALONE. IT PREFERS TO HANG OUT WITH ITS HERD.

*NOTE: A JATOM IS THE SIZE OF JAMIE OR TOM: 4 FT TALL AND 60 LBS IN WEIGHT.
**NOTE: SCIENTISTS CALL THIS PERIOD THE LATE CRETACEOUS.

Landslips where
clay and fossils are

Muddy beach

DINO CAVE

High tide beach line

Low tide beach line

Sea

Smugglers' Point

Jamie Morgan stared at the huge dinosaur towering over him.

"That is awesome!" he exclaimed to his best friend, Tom. "A life-size model of an edmontosaurus skeleton."

The gigantic skeleton barely fit in the museum on the ground floor of Jamie's lighthouse home. Its huge tail curled around the whitewashed walls and it reared up so that its duck-billed nose was high

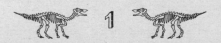

over the boys' heads. The museum was finally
ready.

A big banner hung outside the lighthouse:

Dinosaur Cove Museum
Grand Opening Today
One O'Clock

This was the day everyone had been
waiting for.

FLASH! FLASH! FLASH!

Jamie and Tom blinked in surprise. The
photographer from the county paper was
aiming her camera at the edmontosaurus. They
jumped aside.

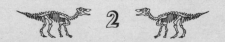

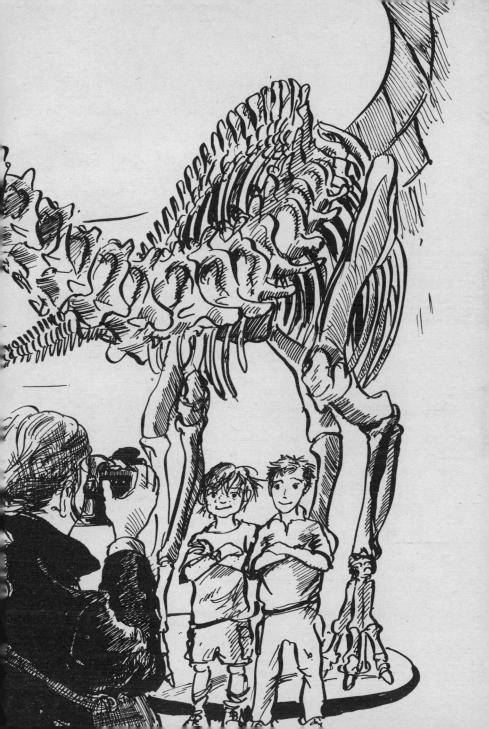

"It's OK, boys," she called, waving an arm. "Let's have you in the shot. It'll show readers just how big this beast really was."

She took picture after picture, then grabbed Jamie's dad and made him pose by the landscape model of the Cretaceous period.

Tom rubbed his eyes. "I'm seeing stars after all that!"

"Imagine how many photos she'd take if she saw a real, live edmontosaurus," said Jamie.

"We've never seen a real one close up," said Tom.

"Maybe we will one day," Jamie whispered.

Jamie and Tom shared an amazing secret. They had discovered Dino World, a land of living dinosaurs, and they visited it whenever they could.

"I wonder why we haven't already seen one," said Tom.

"This will tell us where to look," declared

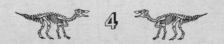

Jamie. He turned on his Fossil Finder and typed in: *EDMONTOSAURUS*.

HERBIVORE, he read from the screen. *ATE LEAVES AND BRANCHES. SLOW MOVING. WALKED ON ITS BACK LEGS* — "Just like our model."

"But where did it live?" asked Tom.

"It says here it kept to the trees to hide from predators. That was its only defense."

"That explains why we've never seen one," said Tom, "if they were always hiding. That should be our next dinosaur mission — hunt the eddie!"

Jamie put the Fossil Finder away in his backpack. He had a gleam in his eye. "Maybe I could ask if we can have a break."

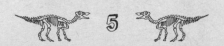

Tom grinned. "Are you thinking what I'm thinking?"

"Time for a trip to Dino World!"

Dad was being photographed next to the triceratops skull so Jamie and Tom ran up to Jamie's grandfather. He was frowning at his reflection in a display case.

"Look at me," he said, before Jamie had a chance to speak. "Why can't I wear my old sweater and pants like I do every other day of the year? I feel silly all dressed up like this."

"But you look so good in that suit, Grandpa," said Jamie. "No one will look at the exhibits. They'll all be admiring you."

Jamie's grandfather laughed as he straightened his tie. "They'll just think I'm another fossil. Now what are you two scamps after? Out with it."

"It's nothing really," said Jamie casually. "It's just that, well, the museum's ready now so we were wondering if we could go outside for a while."

Jamie's grandfather looked at the ankylosaurus-shaped clock on the wall, showing nine fifteen. "Don't see why not," he said. "As long as you're back at one sharp for the ceremony — clean and tidy."

"Thanks, Grandpa." Jamie swung his backpack onto his back and hurried out of the lighthouse, Tom right behind him.

They scrambled across the beach and up to the cave entrance high in the cliffs.

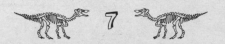

Making sure no one was in sight, they slipped inside. Jamie dug in his backpack for his flashlight, but his hand closed around something lumpy and hard.

"Hey, look," Jamie said, pulling it out along with the flashlight. "This is the ammonite I found on my first day in Dinosaur Cove."

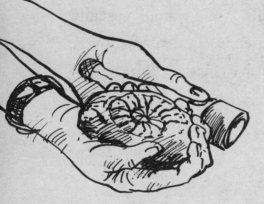

"The first day we discovered Dino World," Tom remembered. Jamie tossed the fossil in his backpack and shone the flashlight on the five fossilized footprints in the stone floor. Every time he saw them he felt the same rush of excitement.

"Let's get back there," he said. The boys trod in each of the dinosaur prints.

One . . . two . . . three . . . four . . . FIVE!

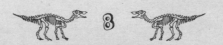

The dark cave disappeared and they stepped into the scorching heat and dazzling light of Dino World.

"It's great to be back!" exclaimed Tom, looking at the huge trees and dense jungle undergrowth around them.

Instead of the usual hum of insects and distant calls of dinosaurs, there was an eerie silence.

"Listen!" Jamie said.

Tom listened hard. "I can't hear a thing."

"Exactly," said Jamie. "Something's not right."

CHAPTER 2

"**W**anna!" called Jamie. His voice sounded strange, echoing through the silent trees. "Where are you, Wanna?"

There was no sign of the friendly little dinosaur who usually came to greet them. The boys began searching the undergrowth, pushing aside the giant tangled vines.

There was a rustling in a nearby laurel bush. "What was that?" Jamie stopped. "Wanna?"

The little wannanosaurus crept out from between the leaves, his eyes darting about nervously. Jamie and Tom rushed over and hugged him.

"You don't know how pleased we are to see you," said Tom, scratching him hard on his scaly back.

But Wanna just gave a feeble grunt.

Tom frowned. "This isn't like you, Wanna. What's the matter?"

Jamie reached up into a tree and picked some orange fruit. "I know what you need, boy," he said. He tossed one to Wanna and put the others in his backpack.

Wanna looked warily around and then gulped the fruit.

"One thing hasn't changed," said Jamie. "Wanna still loves ginkgoes."

"Another thing hasn't changed," Tom said, holding his nose. "The ginkgoes are still as smelly as ever."

"But everything else is different." Jamie frowned. "Let's find out what's going on."

With Wanna sticking close to their heels, they made their way through the jungle to a gap in the trees where they could look out over the Great Plains. The plains lay below them, shimmering in the heat — completely deserted.

"There should be herds of triceratops

and hadrosaurs and lots more," said Tom in disbelief. "I don't like it." He pulled out his binoculars and scanned the plains. "There's nothing moving at all, except the geyser spouts, of course. They're still shooting up into the air."

"What if the dinosaurs are gone?" whispered Jamie.

Tom looked at him, horrified. "No, they must be here somewhere."

The boys started down the steep slope of Ginkgo Hill, but Wanna hung back, trembling and grunting anxiously.

"Come on, boy," called Jamie, holding out a ginkgo from his bag.

The little dinosaur crept forward and ate the fruit. He didn't leave their side as they trampled through the hot, damp under-growth and jumped the stepping-stones over the river.

"This silence is really strange," said Jamie in a low voice.

"And I've never seen Wanna like this before," said Tom. "Not even when we met the T-Rex!"

Suddenly, there was a deafening crash overhead.

BANG!

The boys ducked instinctively.

BANG! Another one. The boys

dived to the ground, covering their heads

15

with their hands. Wanna disappeared under a
cluster of spiky flowers.

Jamie raised his head. "There's no way that
was a dinosaur!" he whispered. "Not even a
T-Rex could make that much noise."

"So what could it be?" Tom asked.

CHAPTER 3

Jamie and Tom scrambled to their feet. "We've got to find out what that was," muttered Jamie. "Here, Wanna!"

A terrified Wanna crept out from the leaves of his hiding place. The three friends walked through the last few trees and out onto the plains.

"Look at that!" Tom gasped.

Two blinding lights, as bright as the sun, were scorching through the sky over the Far Away Mountains.

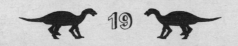

"Meteors!" Jamie gasped, screening his eyes from the glare.

The boys watched as the glowing objects shot toward the middle of the plains like supersonic jets. They left long, dazzling trails behind them.

"They're falling to Earth!" yelled Jamie. "And fast."

"They're going to hit the plains," shouted Tom.

BOOM!
BOOM!

There was a dreadful noise like cannon fire. The ground shook and the boys and Wanna were knocked off their feet.

The trees behind them shuddered wildly. All at once the sky was full of pterosaurs, screeching and squawking, and there were calls from the jungle — deep and rumbling. Out on the plains, two columns of dust billowed into the air where the meteors had hit.

Jamie and Tom sat up. Wanna was still lying on his back, shaking.

"Cool!" said Jamie. "We've just seen a meteor strike!"

"And felt it!" said Tom, getting up and gently pulling Wanna to his feet. "No wonder he was so nervous and all the dinosaurs are hiding. They must have sensed the danger."

The boys scanned the plains from Fang Rock right around to the cliffs of the White Ocean. There were still no creatures to be seen. Even the pterosaurs had disappeared again.

A look of horror came over Tom's face. "Don't some people say that it was a meteor that killed the dinosaurs millions of years ago? Do you think that's going to happen here?"

"No," said Jamie firmly. "That one was so huge that it created a massive dust cloud and blocked out the sun. These haven't. But we can find out more about them." He pulled out his Fossil Finder and tapped in: *METEOR*. Then he read, *A LUMP OF ROCK FROM SPACE THAT HITS EARTH'S ATMOSPHERE WITH A SONIC BOOM . . .*

"That must have been the bangs we heard when we were in the jungle." Tom nodded.

AND STREAKS ACROSS THE SKY WITH A BRIGHT GLOW, Jamie continued. *THE ONES THAT HIT THE EARTH ARE CALLED METEORITES.*

He turned the Fossil Finder toward Tom. "Look: Here are some awesome pictures."

"Wow!" Tom said. "We could actually see real meteorites — just after they'd landed!"

"I've always wanted to see a space rock," said Jamie. "Let's head for those dust clouds."

The boys left the jungle behind them and set off across the vast, grassy plains. Wanna scampered along, looking happier now.

"They've landed a lot farther away than I thought," said Tom. "One of the dust clouds is right at the foot of the Far Away Mountains — near that forest."

"Then we'll head for the closer one," said Jamie, "near where the geysers are." He pulled out the map they'd made of Dino World. "That's where we chased the velociraptor."

"Well, I hope he's not still lurking around!" Tom checked his compass. "We should head northwest," he said.

"Shouldn't we be seeing the geysers gushing up?" Jamie shielded his eyes as he peered forward.

"The dust must be hiding them," said Tom.

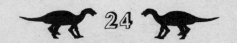

He held an imaginary microphone.
"And here's Tom Clay taking
you on a quest to find the
supersonic space
rocks that have
spooked all the
creatures of
Dino World."

"I wonder what
Tom Clay has to
say about the ground
ahead," Jamie said,
pointing.

"It's black!" Tom gasped. "I
mean . . . Now we can clearly see
the effects of this meteorite strike.
We are entering the blast area now.
All around the vegetation is singed
and . . . Wow! I can feel the heat
through my sneakers."

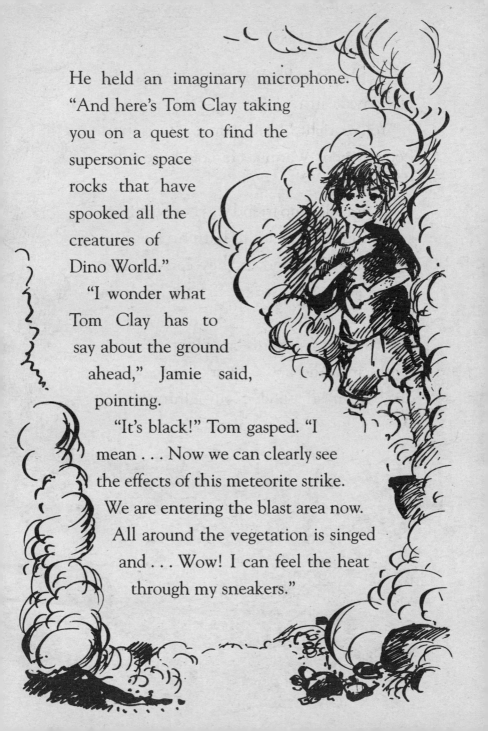

The boys walked gingerly across the blackened earth.

"You're right," said Jamie. "It is hot! Look at poor Wanna. He could use some shoes."

Their little dino friend was hopping from side to side, trying not to burn his feet.

"Look!" Tom said as they came nearer to the site of the strike. "There are little fires all around us."

Small plants were crackling, sending sparks into the air. A spark landed on a dry bush nearby and it burst into flames. Wanna skittered off in alarm.

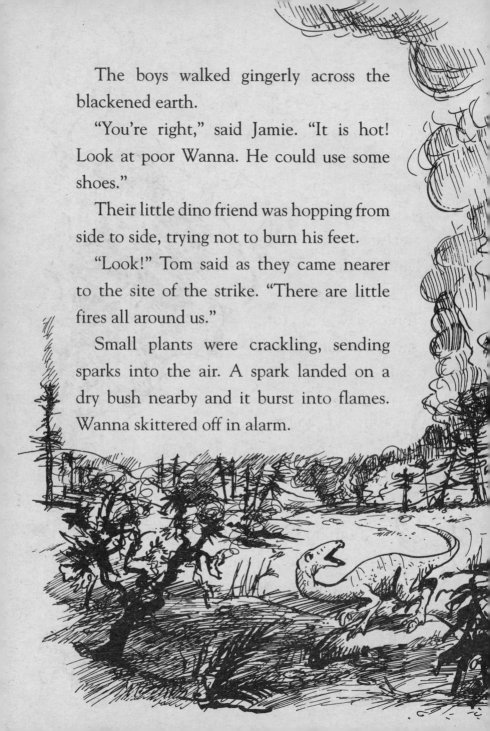

"It's OK, Wanna," said Tom. "Stick with us and you'll be fine."

"The fires will probably have scared off the raptor," Jamie guessed.

"Good thing for us, because we don't have any bacon to distract it," Tom said.

The air was becoming very dusty.

"We should have reached the geysers by now," said Jamie. "But why can't we hear the water spouting?"

Cautiously,
the boys stepped
forward and saw a huge,
gaping hole.

"This is where the geysers should be,"
Tom said.

They peered over the rim of the pit
and Jamie's feet dislodged stones, which
tumbled into the bottomless dark.
They could hear hissing and rumbling
deep underground.

"It's like being on the edge of a cliff," gasped Tom. "The ground's just . . . vanished!"

"The meteorite destroyed the geysers," said Jamie in amazement.

"That's some power," said Tom. "It must have smashed through the underground caverns where the water heats up. Now the geysers can't spout anymore."

"The hole looks as wide as a football field," said Jamie. "And who knows how deep."

Grunk-shoo!

Wanna was sniffing at the edge, sneezing as the steam went up his nose. There was a sound of shifting stones and the ground beneath his feet began to crumble. Earth spilled down into the darkness.

"Get back, Wanna!" cried Tom in alarm. "It's not safe."

But it was too late. With a horrible crack, the edge gave way. Wanna didn't even have time to grunk before he disappeared into the deep, cavernous hole.

"Wanna!" yelled Tom.

CHAPTER 4

Jamie dropped to his hands and knees and edged toward the place where Wanna had disappeared. He felt the hot steam on his face as he peered into the blackness. Had they lost their faithful friend?

"Wanna?" Jamie called out tentatively into the dark chasm.

Grunk. The response was soft and frightened, but relief flooded through Jamie. Wanna was still alive!

"I can see him!" Jamie yelled. "He's stuck on a sort of rock shelf."

"We've got to rescue him!" Tom exclaimed.

Jamie took off his backpack and lay down on his stomach. "I'll try to reach him."

Tom held his friend's ankles as Jamie leaned carefully over the hole. Through the steam Jamie could just see Wanna, cowering on the ledge, his eyes wide and terrified. Beyond him was nothing but the dark of the deep, steaming pit.

Quick as lightning, Jamie made a grab for him. His fingers closed around one front leg. "Got him!"

He felt Tom pulling hard on his ankles as Jamie clung to Wanna with all his strength. Wanna scrabbled on the side of the rock wall, trying to help. Slowly and surely, Jamie and Tom hauled Wanna up out of the pit. At last, the three of them lay sprawled on the ground.

"That was close," Tom said.

The little dinosaur darted between his rescuers, licking their faces.

"I think he's saying thank you." Jamie grinned.

Grunk, grunk!

Wanna seemed to agree.

"We're not going to find any meteorites in that steam hole," said Tom. "Let's check out the other landing site." He pointed to the dust

cloud, that was still hovering over the trees at the foot of the Far Away Mountains.

"We haven't been that way before," said Jamie. "We'll be able to add what we find to the map."

"Good idea," said Tom, checking his compass. "We're heading north of the geysers, or what's left of them."

Skirting carefully around the huge pit, the boys set off with Wanna, heading straight toward the Far Away Mountains. As they got closer, the ground became rougher. They had to step over big rocks to reach the blackened earth of the second strike. More plants were crackling around them, and they could see that the trees nestling at the foot of the mountains had been scorched by the blast.

There were small fires burning among the broken branches.

"On with our mission," said Jamie. "Meteorite, here we come."

"There's the crater," said Tom. He pointed to a dip in the ground about twenty yards ahead.

"Yay!" Jamie hurried toward it. It was a perfect saucer shape. In the center lay a jagged black rock, glinting in the sun.

Jamie punched the air. "It's the meteorite!"

They slid down the gentle slope to the gleaming space rock.

"Awesome!" Tom cheered.

Jamie gingerly reached out a finger to touch the surface. "It's cold!" he said in surprise. He flicked open the Fossil Finder. METEORITES, he read. FRAGMENTS OF ROCK THAT FALL TO EARTH FROM SPACE. THEY RANGE IN SIZE FROM A GRAIN OF SAND UP TO A FOOTBALL STADIUM.

"Wow!" Tom gasped. "I'm glad this one's not as big as that!" He tried to lift it but it didn't budge. "It's amazing that it's cold when everything else around here is scorched."

Jamie scanned his Fossil Finder. "It says the meteorite is only hot when it enters the atmosphere and will have cooled down by the time it reaches the ground. The fires around are caused by the impact when it hits."

They examined the rock closely. "It's got shiny pieces of metal in it," said Tom, running his hand over it. "And holes like space worms have burrowed through it."

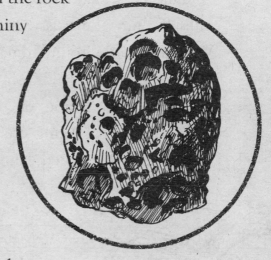

"Just think," said Jamie, jumping on top of the rock. "Less than an hour ago this was hurtling through the galaxy!"

Tom joined him. "Here's Tom Clay and Jamie Morgan, famous explorers, whizzing past the stars on their own personal meteor."

"Whoa! There goes Mars!"

"Watch the moon!"

"Here comes planet Earth. *Crash!*"

Jamie jumped off the meteorite and threw himself onto the dusty floor of the crater. Wanna grunked around him, enjoying the fun.

"I'm off to Saturn!" Tom announced from the meteorite. "Hang on, what's that?" he said seriously, balancing on tiptoe. "I can see a dinosaur!" He asked Jamie to pass up the binoculars and then peered toward the distant trees, which were still smoldering from the meteor strike.

Jamie climbed up beside him. "What is it?"

Tom handed him the binoculars. "Take a look."

Jamie aimed them at the trees. "Wow!" He focused on a flat, wide dinosaur head with a beak-shaped snout and let out a low whistle. "It's an edmontosaurus — a real, live one!"

CHAPTER 5

Jamie scrambled out of the crater and swept the binoculars along the line of trees. "There's a whole herd of edmontosauruses!" he exclaimed. "They're massive!"

"Cool," Tom said, hurrying to join him.

The great lumbering dinosaurs were huddled together at the edge of the forest. They took nervous steps on their hind legs toward the smoldering trees and then skittered back in alarm.

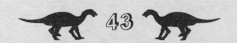

"But they don't belong in the open." Tom looked worried. "That forest must be their home."

"Looks like they're too scared to go back in," said Jamie. "Some of those branches are still on fire."

He trained the binoculars on an edmontosaurus at the edge of the group and chuckled. "I think that one's posing for us!"

The eddie lifted up its head and sniffed the air. It opened its mouth, showing rows and rows of flat teeth.

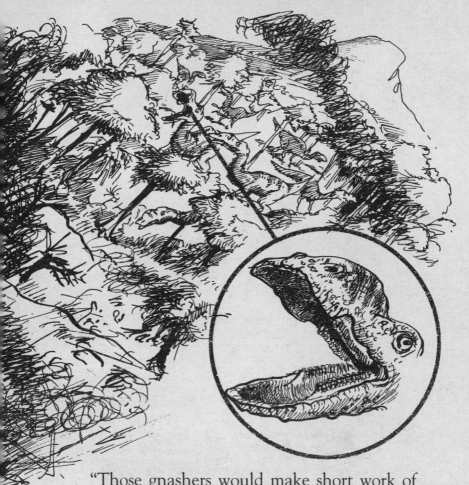

"Those gnashers would make short work of
a tree branch," Jamie murmured. "Dad told me
they could have up to a thousand teeth!"

"I wouldn't like to be a dino dentist." Tom
laughed. "You'd need a drill the size of a
baseball bat."

"And buckets of mouthwash."

"And half your patients would want to eat you!"

"I wish we could get a bit closer," said Jamie. "Do we have time?"

Tom looked at his watch. "Not really. We'd better go. We'll be in big trouble if we're late getting back for the grand opening. Come on, Wanna."

They began the long walk back toward the geyser crater and the jungle beyond.

"I wish we could tell Dad that we've seen

some real edmontosauruses." Jamie sighed. He turned to get one last look at the eddies and stopped dead.

"Oh, no!" he said. "Look at the flames! The whole forest is on fire now!"

Fierce flames were shooting up into the sky from the treetops.

"The eddies don't like it," said Tom, "and I don't blame them. Their home's burning."

The dinosaurs were backing off from the trees, buffeting each other in their fear. The boys could hear their deep, anxious calls.

Suddenly, a flaming tree trunk crashed down, hitting the ground in a shower of sparks.

With a terrified bellow, the herd reared away and began to run from the burning trees. Soon the run became a charge. The ground churned under their pounding feet and dust flew up around them.

"They're stampeding," yelled Tom. "And they're heading right for us."

"We better get out of the way, and fast," Jamie said. "Come on, Wanna!"

The boys and their dinosaur friend sprinted back the way they had come, trying to put some distance between themselves and the frightened dinosaurs. Soon they

had to dodge the small fires
that still burned here and there in
the blast area from the first meteorite.

Jamie turned to see if the eddies were still
stampeding toward them. "Wait a minute!" he
shouted. "If the eddies keep running this way,
they'll fall into the geyser pit."

Tom slowed down, panting. "We can't let
that happen!"

"We've got to stop them or turn them away
somehow," said Jamie.

"We could wave our T-shirts at them," Tom
suggested.

"Too small," answered Jamie.

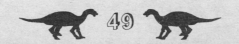

"But we don't have anything else," Tom said, worried.

"Yes, we do," said Jamie, running over to a burning bush. "We'll use fire. That's what scared them into stampeding in the first place. We'll stand in front of the pit and wave burning branches."

"Brilliant!" said Tom. "Let's do it."

Wanna butted their legs, as if to keep them away from the danger.

"No, Wanna," said Jamie. "We've got to do this." He broke off two crackling branches and held them high. Wanna backed away, grunting in alarm. "Sorry, little friend,"

he said soothingly, "but it's up to us to save the eddies."

The boys rushed over to the pit, then turned and faced the oncoming charge.

Jamie could feel sparks from the burning branches stinging his arms, but he wasn't going to give up. The terrified edmontosauruses were thundering toward them, churning up the dust.

The drumming of giant feet was making the ground shudder. Jamie looked over his shoulder to see a large crack appear near his feet.

CRASH!

A great chunk of earth disappeared into the darkness. Now the edge of the pit was right behind them. If the crack got any wider, the boys would fall into the pit themselves.

"The eddies have to stop!" shouted Jamie desperately. "It's their only chance — and ours!"

CHAPTER 6

Jamie and Tom waved the burning branches as hard as they could.

But the edmontosauruses were surging on, pounding away on all fours. They were so close, the boys could see their eyes, wide with fear, and their nostrils flaring in panic.

"It's not working," cried Tom.

"We can't give up!" Jamie shouted.

The stampeding herd was only yards away now. Was it too late? Were they all going to plunge into the crater?

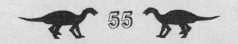

"STOP!" Jamie and Tom bellowed desperately.

At the last minute, the eddies seemed to notice the fire. The leading dinosaurs reared up in terror and swerved away from the geyser pit. The rest of the herd followed, thundering past, throwing dust into the boys' faces.

"We saved them!" yelled Tom.

Grunk, grunk! Wanna appeared and scampered over.

"I agree, Wanna," Jamie said. "That was close."

"Those eddies used all four legs to gallop," said Tom. "No wonder they were moving so fast."

"That's what we'd better do," said Jamie, looking at his watch, "if we're going to be on time for the grand opening."

They hurried back toward the jungle. Wanna was his old self, scurrying between

them, running ahead and grunking happily all
the time.

"At least we got to see a real meteorite," said
Jamie. "And you got your wish, Tom."

"What was that?" Tom was puzzled.

"You wanted to see an edmontosaurus close
up, remember?"

"I didn't mean *that* close!" Tom grinned.

They climbed back up Ginkgo Hill.
Wanna waggled his tail in delight as they
went.

"He knows there'll be a nice treat
waiting for him," Tom added.

When they reached the cave, they took one more look out over Dino World. A herd of triceratops was grazing by the lagoon and hadrosaurs were plodding down to the river by Fang Rock. Pterosaurs lazily circled in the air. They all seemed to know that the danger was over.

"We can't forget to change our map when we get back," said Tom. "The geysers are gone and there's that new crater. And the eddies' trees, of course."

Jamie took the binoculars and focused on the eddies' trees, which were still burning. "I hope the fire doesn't spread or we'll be making even more changes."

"I don't think it will," said Tom. "Look." Away in the distance, storm clouds were gathering over the mountains. "The rain will soon put the fire out."

The boys hurried into the cave and Wanna followed.

Grunk, grunk! Wanna stared at them sadly for a moment, as if he didn't want them to go.

"Don't worry, Wanna," Tom said, patting him on his hard head. "We'll be back soon."

Jamie gave him the last of the ginkgoes and Wanna cheered up, gobbling up the treats. Jamie and Tom waved good-bye and stepped backward into the dinosaur footprints and found themselves back in Dinosaur Cove. They scrambled down to the beach.

Then Tom stopped. "We can't go to the grand opening like this. We're filthy."

"You're right. Grandpa will have a fit," said Jamie, "and I don't know what Dad will do — explode probably."

"Quick," said Tom. "We can wash ourselves off in the sea."

They hurriedly scrubbed the grime off their arms, legs, and faces and made a dash for the lighthouse. The distant church clock was striking one.

It looked as if the whole village had come to the grand opening, and crowds of tourists, too. A line stretched down the path.

"Our clothes will have to do," muttered Jamie as they made their way past the line of people. "We've got no more time. Hopefully, everyone will be too busy looking at the museum to notice."

Then they heard a loud voice. "That edmontosaurus would be an easy target!" A fifteen-year-old boy was looking at a poster for the museum showing the eddie model. He seemed to be telling his friend all about dinosaurs. "They were slow plodders, believe me. Anything could eat them if they wanted. Bet they couldn't run."

"Are you sure?" his friend asked.

"Of course I'm sure," said the boy. "I know everything there is to know about dinosaurs."

Tom looked at Jamie. "You tell him," he whispered.

"Excuse me," said Jamie politely. "But the edmontosaurus could get up quite a speed by running on all four legs. It wasn't always an easy target."

"How do you know?" demanded the boy.

"I've seen —" Jamie stopped himself and quickly recovered. "I've seen the edmontosaurus skeleton inside. Have a look when you go in. Its front limbs were definitely long enough to run on."

The boy stared at him openmouthed.

Tom saw Jamie's grandfather waving them over. The boys marched up to the front of the crowd and up onto the little stage to stand with Jamie's dad.

"Welcome to the Dinosaur Cove Museum," Mr. Morgan began. "The most magical dinosaur place in the whole world . . ."

Jamie smiled a huge smile. He was proud of his dad's new museum, but it was nothing compared to Dino World.

"The second most magical place," Jamie whispered to Tom.

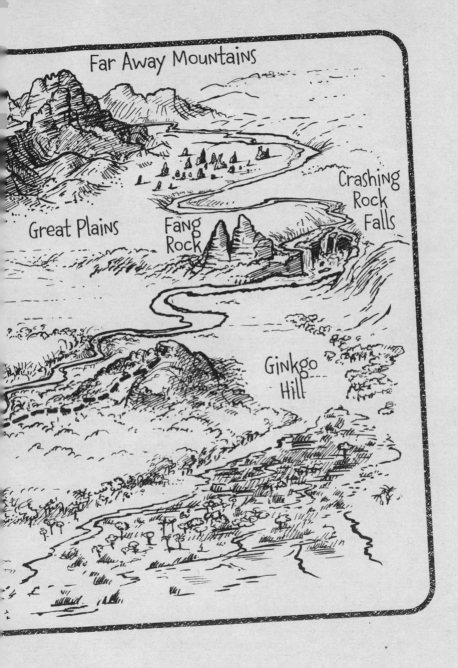

GLOSSARY

Ammonite — an extinct animal with octopuslike legs and often a spiral-shaped shell that lived in the ocean.

Edmontosaurus — a plant-eating, usually slow-moving dinosaur that walked on its back two legs. Named after the place where it was discovered in southern Alberta, Canada, once called "Lower Edmonton."

Geyser — a hot spring, heated by volcanic activity below the earth's surface, that erupts in a tall stream of hot water and steam, sometimes on a regular schedule.

Ginkgo — a tree native to China called a "living fossil" because fossils of it have been found dating back millions of years, yet they are still around today. Also known as the stink bomb tree because of its smelly apricotlike fruit.

Hadrosaur — a duck-billed dinosaur. This plant eater had a toothless beak but hundreds of teeth in its cheeks.

Meteor — matter from outer space that glows when falling through the earth's atmosphere.

Meteorite — a meteor that lands on the earth's surface.

Pterosaur — a prehistoric flying reptile. Its wings were leathery and light, and some of these "winged lizards" had fur on their bodies and bony crests on their heads.

Triceratops (T-tops) — a three-horned, plant-eating dinosaur that looked like a rhinoceros.

Wannanosaurus — a dinosaur that only ate plants and used its hard, flat skull to defend itself. Named after the place where it was discovered: Wannano, in China.

COME AND MEET ME ...
IN A JURASSIC ADVENTURE

Read all of Tom and Jamie's dinosaur adventures

Don't miss Dinosaur Cove's T-Rex, Triceratops, Velociraptor, and the other fearsome creatures of the Cretaceous!

And for a journey into the Jurassic, check out

DINOSAUR COVE #7: SAVING THE STEGOSAURUS